Periwinkle Smith

and the Twirly, Whirly Tutu

For Sarah and Kate—Periwinkle Smith's
first and best friends.

Periwinkle Smith

and the Twirly, Whirly Tutu

by John & Wendy

PSS!
PRICE STERN SLOAN

Periwinkle Smith loved her twirly, whirly white tutu.

She loved to **JuMP,**

twirl,

and

Pirouette

in it.

She never wanted to take it off.

Not when she went to the park.

Not when she
played games.

Not when she went to bed.

Not even when
she painted.

And she *loved*
to paint.

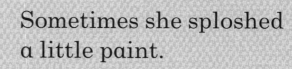

Sometimes she sploshed
a little paint.

Sometimes on her
pirate hat.

Sometimes on her
monkey chair.

Her bedroom was covered in spots.

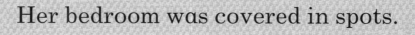

With the Big Pink Spot
on her flouncy, bouncy white tutu,

Periwinkle couldn't even *think* about jumping, twirling, or pirouetting.

She tried to wash it out.

She tried to rub it out.

Even spot remover was a *not*-remover.

She tried to scare it away,
but it was too brave.

Roar!

She tried to magic it away,
but it was too powerful.

She tried to hide it.

She tried to ignore it.

But she knew it was there.

If she couldn't dance in her tutu,
what *could* she do with it?

She tried to turn it into a kite,
but it wouldn't fly.

She tried to dress up her cat,
but he wouldn't play along.

The Big Pink Spot was all Periwinkle Smith could think about!

Just then she spotted more spots.

Suddenly, Periwinkle
began to see spots
in a *new* way.

She got out her paints . . .

. . . and the Big Pink Spot
became a Big Pink Flower!

(With lots of little flower friends
to keep it company, of course.)

Periwinkle's spotty, dotty, colorful tutu made her want to

JUMP,

PRICE STERN SLOAN
Published by the Penguin Group
Penguin Group (USA) Inc., 375 Hudson Street, New York, New York 10014, USA
Penguin Group (Canada), 90 Eglinton Avenue East, Suite 700,
Toronto, Ontario M4P 2Y3, Canada
(a division of Pearson Penguin Canada Inc.)
Penguin Books Ltd., 80 Strand, London WC2R 0RL, England
Penguin Group Ireland, 25 St. Stephen's Green, Dublin 2, Ireland
(a division of Penguin Books Ltd.)
Penguin Group (Australia), 250 Camberwell Road, Camberwell,
Victoria 3124, Australia
(a division of Pearson Australia Group Pty. Ltd.)
Penguin Books India Pvt. Ltd., 11 Community Centre,
Panchsheel Park, New Delhi—110 017, India
Penguin Group (NZ), 67 Apollo Drive, Rosedale, North Shore 0632, New Zealand
(a division of Pearson New Zealand Ltd.)
Penguin Books (South Africa) (Pty.) Ltd., 24 Sturdee Avenue,
Rosebank, Johannesburg 2196, South Africa

Penguin Books Ltd., Registered Offices: 80 Strand, London WC2R 0RL, England